Dear Mom

Volume I

Ukiyoto Publishing

All global publishing rights are held by

Ukiyoto Publishing

Published in 2023

Content Copyright © Ukiyoto

ISBN 9789360162931

All rights reserved.
No part of this publication may be reproduced, transmitted, or stored in a retrieval system, in any form by any means, electronic, mechanical, photocopying, recording or otherwise, without the prior permission of the publisher.

The moral rights of the author have been asserted.

This is a work of fiction. Names, characters, businesses, places, events, locales, and incidents are either the products of the author's imagination or used in a fictitious manner. Any resemblance to actual persons, living or dead, or actual events is purely coincidental.

This book is sold subject to the condition that it shall not by way of trade or otherwise, be lent, resold, hired out or otherwise circulated, without the publisher's prior consent, in any form of binding or cover other than that in which it is published.

www.ukiyoto.com

Contents

Poems and Short Story by Pabitra Adhikary	1
Short Story by Tamikio L. Dooley	12
Short Story and Poems by Imelda Valisto Caravaca	19
Short Story by Dante Villanueva Aguilar	32
Short Story by Maitrayee Banerjee	43
Poem by Riddhima Sen	49
Poem by Nivedita Bhattacharya	52
Poem by Quinn Jam	57
Short Story by R. Chaitanya	72
About the Authors	*79*

Poems and Short Story by Pabitra Adhikary

Dedicated To My Mom

Mom I am indebted to you,
So profusely obligated that
Perhaps I can never repay your debt.

The memory of the countless moments spent with you
Give me the inspiration to live.

The Mother Beyond Comparison

Mom, you are not there,
So, I feel lonely even among the billions of people of the world.
It seems that
There is no one to shower that special affection to me.

Only a mother can feed her child remaining half-fed herself.
It is a Mother's care and affection that
Make her wake up at midnight and wrap her shivering child with a blanket,
Mothers can do wonders.

A little conversation or thought-sharing with Mother
During the times of worries and anxieties,
Makes the mind peaceful;
All tensions are released
Within seconds.

Now that you are not here, Mom,
I keep all my sorrow, pain and sufferings to myself,
There is no one to share my agonies with.

I was very loyal to my mother right from childhood,
However, she fulfilled many of my unfair demands

cheerfully and with a smiling face.
As a child, I used to ask her, "Mom, I feel like eating this or that today. Will you please cook it for me?"
Now, there is no one to ask for such pampering.

After a five-year-long fight with the deadly disease of cancer
My mother left for her heavenly abode.
I could not save her life;
I tried to console my grief-stricken mind by thinking that
It is nature's rule that whoever is born has to leave this world one day.

Mom, I am indebted to you,
So profusely obligated that
Perhaps I can never repay your debt.

The memory of the countless moments spent with you
Give me the inspiration to live.

Mother is the most beautiful word in this world,
Mothers are beyond comparison,
Mothers are the God-gifted icons of love.
We must learn from our Mothers
How to compromise everything for love, how to love selflessly.

In my view, women are the symbols of motherhood.
I have found a great mother within every woman,
Sometimes it is apparent and sometimes subtle.
That is why I consider women the source of creation.
I respect women,
They hold a precious position in my mind.

The Pathetic Narrative of a Venerable Mother

I am a village boy. So, I had no concept about the old age home. Ever since I was a child, I had settled my parents above God.

Every parent gives their all to rear a kid. Instead of fulfilling their hobbies and amusements, they aspire for a stronger future for their children with their last resources. Parents have to give up a lot to take care of their infants.

Those parents should not be dropped in the old age home as soon as their demands are matched. The child must take care of every elderly parent. This moral instruction must be demonstrated to every child.

Almighty God may be the one who offers the children the dignity they deserve. There is no benefit in worshipping God by ignoring one's parents. The room of the old parents is the real temple.

Parents, family and the surroundings play a vital role in developing the personality of any toddler. Remember, whatever we undertake today, our offspring will pursue in the future. If we show due respect to our aged parents, our future generations will provide us honour in the future.

Remember, there is nothing more precious in this universe than a parent's blessing. A parent's grace is more valuable than all treasures. In a household where parents are not provided due respect, the family will never be happy.

I came to study in Kolkata. I lived as a paying guest. The proprietor of the house, uncle and aunt, lived on the second floor, and I remained in a room on the first floor. Their son Abir and their son's wife Payel both worked in Mumbai. Uncle and aunt loved me like their own son.

Soumitra Babu, our next-door neighbour, died of a heart attack on Sunday night. I was deeply perturbed to hear.

His age was more than 60. He was an extremely lively gentleman. He came to visit me several times by himself. He was somewhat concerned about my studies.

Two days afterwards, on Tuesday morning, there was a conversation between son Anirban and daughter-in-law Swastika.

Son Anirban worked in a high position in the bank, daughter-in-law Swastika was a modern homemaker, but she had no enthusiasm for housekeeping. Anirban's seven-year-old son Abhik was now in class two in the most prestigious convent school in Kolkata.

Swastika said, "Look, I can't see your sick mom. I've accomplished a lot, I can't go on anymore. It is not my obligation to look at your mom. Get your mother out of this house the day after your father's obsequies."

Anirban said, "Don't talk like this. Now if I send my mother to an old age home, what will the neighbours say?"

Swastika said, "So? I can't listen to the neighbour. I require peace in my life. I can't stand so much trouble anymore."

Anirban said, "As you suggested, I have fixed three workmen in the morning, at noon, and in the night too. Please, try to accommodate mother a slight."

Swastika said, "I can't. Do not always point out the term, three workmen, repeatedly. Do you know how much activity there is at home? Have you ever supported me with housekeeping? The child is now in second grade. Do you know how much time I have to spend on his studies? Never underrate the employment of a housewife."

Anirban said, "But my mom used to deal with the whole housework alone without any workman."

Swastika said, "You know, your mother spoiled you completely. Your mother's generation was different, today's era is distinctive. You go and relax in the office all day, what responsibility do we have at home, what do you understand? Is the house mine alone? The household is for both of us. So, both of us should do the housework equally. But your mother did not teach you that. She has devoured your full brain. It is not my business to look at your mom. I've worked out a lot, and I can't. You have to resolve now whether you will choose me or your sick mother."

Anirban said, "I'll see. Please, allow me time to consider."

The next day, Soumitra Babu's daughter Shrabanti was called.

She arrived and delivered the same answer. "Brother and sister-in-law will enjoy the father's apartment. Will I see the sick mother? Do you assume I'm stupid?"

Swastika said, "We have seen mother for so long. So now I demand to dispatch mother to the old age home."

Shrabanti said, "Do whatever you wish. But don't get me in trouble."

Soumitra Babu's wife Madhabilata might not have heard these points as he could hear very little in the ear. Maybe she was pretending not to hear everything. I couldn't stand watching him helplessly like this.

Her face resembled a lot like my grandmother Lakshmishree.

On the day of Soumitra Babu's obsequies, I was also invited along with uncle and aunt. Lots of foodstuffs were arranged there. Before that, I hadn't seen so much food during the mourning period in a household.

Aunty said in front of everyone that day, "Anirban, I think you are like my own son. Don't send your mom to an old age home. She hears less, never stays out of the residence."

Before Anirban could explain anything, Swastika said, "Don't provoke him like this. Now I have all the authority over him. Another point, I don't like sniffing in other people's business."

Everyone became mute. Uncle told aunty to be relaxed.

I was very indignant with Anirban Babu. There was nothing improper with listening to your spouse. My dad also talked to my mother first before making any judgement. Then he used to take any decision. But listening to his wife's words, Anirban Babu was doing injustice to his mother, which was not desirable of encouragement at all. No child should treat the mother this way.

The era has changed.

That night, uncle called his son and said, "Mom called you yesterday. Didn't you talk for a minute? It's been going on for a long time. But your mother is truly depressed."

Abir replied, "Sorry dad. I was extremely busy for a few days, so I am calling my mom right now."

That's when Abir called and talked to aunty for about thirty minutes. Aunty later revealed to uncle, "Why did you say that to the child? I didn't tell you anything."

Uncle replied, "The mother has to teach the son her likes or dislikes. The era has evolved remarkably. The present generation is overlooking the duty of every child to be by the side of parents at the last age."

The next morning, her son took Madhabilata Debi to the old age home.

Madhabilata Debi was breaking down a lot before leaving. The night before, her daughter and daughter-in-law divided all the jewellery. They had shared them in equal parts. Now Madhabilata Debi became exceedingly poor.

It seemed like it was going to rain very heavily, and then I would have peace of mind.

Then Swastika and her son Abhik were sitting on the verandah of the house. But today, what the convent schoolboy learnt from life would ever be capable of being a true human being? I had apprehensions.

This is how a generation is coming to an end. If he reiterates the same action when he grows up, can he be condemned?

Short Story by Tamikio L. Dooley

My Sisters, Amandla
(Nairobi, Kenya, April 5, 1989)

I am an African black daughter telling my sisters' heroic story about courage, wisdom, and continuity. My sisters—Amandla is the oldest sister of five daughters—are African daughters born in heritage and culture. Behind Amandla's courage, wisdom, and continuity lies endeavours and bumps. I talk about my sisters' way of life as she's an inspiration to us. Where we understand setting boundaries, not growing into whoever's figurine, plucking the strings, we manage our own. Amandla's short inspiring story interweaves strongholds, breaking the chains of our African ancestors. As black women, we struggle in the mind, heart, and soul.

Let me tell you about My Sisters, Amandla.

I say my 'sisters' because we are one and Amandla, our keeper. I know everybody needs to know who I am, singing about my sisters, Amandla. I'm Adwin.

That's who I am. 'Adwin' means an artist, a creative person. 'Aadelheide' means the Estonian form of Alice, meaning noble. 'Aamber' means a precious jewel or gemstone of warm honey colour. 'Aasta' means love. 'Amandla' means a powerful woman; brave and strong. Amandla is more than brave and strong. She's courageous, full of wisdom, and imaginative. 'Ahnika' means ruler of the house and is what our mother's name was. Our names of Africa possess powerful meanings. Naturally, our names mean the greatest prestige. What natural ways do I speak of? Bold, brave, adventurous, full of wisdom and agility. It was the face of our skin that hurt the most. They overlooked our natural ways. I never understood how an individual's skin colour influenced their capability to be human…and to love. We are all made from the same cloth. God created man and woman from dust, which is where we shall return. Our skin colour, our face, shouldn't matter. But to some people, it does. Our mother taught us about love.

We should love everyone. This includes colour, age, culture, and ethically, is who they are. Love is love. Acceptance is acceptance. We are no longer joined to our mother's womb. We bleed the same colour, crimson.

Yes, it's true.

Perhaps it happens when diverse individuals cause us to bleed, spreading anguish and suffering. Because of their personal feelings, their hardhearted beliefs, it is how their parents raised them. They thrive changing someone else's identity. It's a depressing, wretched shame. But we never forgot what our mother taught us. Because of Amandla, we maintained. Because of Amandla, we are bold, full of wisdom, understanding, and heroism. She taught us to build our inner traits. As I mentioned, my name is Adwin. My name means an artist, a creative person. I can take the beautifulness of my name and create love, colour, silhouettes of my youthful learning. I didn't mention our ages. I'm thirty-five-years-born, the youngest of the five sisters. Aadelheide is thirty- six. Aamber is thirty-seven. Aasta is thirty-eight. And Amandla is thirty-nine. We create five-years behind our beauty transformations. My mother was in her mid-fifties. Yes, she 'was,' is what I said.

Our birth mother gave us, in looks, my sisters, Amandla has brown skin, like coffee beans, thick lips, like dark chocolate balls, eyes, like milk duds, and hair, of dreadlocks, embraced in a colourful, flowered scarf. Aasta has dark brown skin, like light, natural highlights, average lips, like lightly tinted, grey eyes, like granite of past struggles, and small forms of dreadlocks, like worms of the earth. Aamber has brown skin, like an acorn, thick lips made of soft pinkish figs, dark brown eyes, like dark coffee beans, and kinky hair, pulled back into a ball in the head's centre. Aadelheide has dark brown skin, light, natural highlights, round, thick lips, with the curves and edges of African roads, light brown eyes, outlined with strong-ship, and kinky, puffy hair, made in an afro. And me, Adwin, with light brown skin, like light, natural highlights, my lips are thick and full, light brown eyes, like amber and caramel, nappy, thick hair, all over my skull.

I've told much about my sisters, Amandla, but haven't said much about our mother, Ahnika, ruler of the house, that she *was*, creating five strong, beautiful daughters, capturing very much of similar qualities.

We were born in strength, not knowing anything about our father. But, we, the daughters, thank him for giving the sperm of life.

Growing up in Nairobi, Kenya, we had to work hard in our mother's land. We had to provide, after she couldn't, provide for her, as well as ourselves. We carried the weight of our baskets, woven baskets, on our heads, backs, and shoulders. Sometimes the carry weighed us down, other days the carry barely settled upon where we chose to carry. Yes, I'm mean, our burdens were inside those baskets amongst many others. Believe it or not, we carried our father's burdens too. There were glorious days when we sipped the taste of wine, when any, but water, very much within our reach. Our region consumes cereals like maize, millets, and sorghum, the staples of the cuisine. We are accompanied with meat and vegetables. Some of the most widely consumed Kenyan dishes are sukuma wiki, a dish made with greens, ugali, cornmeal porridge, and nyama choma, a grilled meat dish. Some of us prefer chicken and ugali meals with vegetables and mursik, a type of fermented milk. Like taro and sweet potatoes and legumes, they are part of the cuisine of the Kikuyu people of Central Kenya. Fish and other seafood are popular in the country's coastal area.

But I can say, not just wine and water fill our souls' born contents, we eat food, much of it, but sometimes that isn't enough. We need our ancestors' struggles and triumphs nourishing our bones acknowledging what they suffered, so we can change the pattern. With the colour of our skin hindering us, it is hard shifting our struggles into triumphs for the sake of our ancestors, because the suffering follows us day and night. Mother taught my sisters and me this. She taught us to first overcome struggles, we have to acknowledge them, look at them, see how they eat away our bones, chipping at our skin, turning us into something we weren't born to become. We support ourselves in our community, the African community, and of course, we welcome any nation outside our skin. Acceptance is the key to healing any community and nation. Pain never goes away. It's about how we answer the call. How we react to the answer. My sisters, Amandla, still teaches us all of this, even after our mother's departure. We stand strong, carrying those woven baskets holding our burdens, pains, and struggles. Our triumph comes not from within the woven baskets, but from the answer, from the call, chipping away our skin, and deteriorating our bones.

The morning our mother lay departed on her bed in the woven tint, just like the baskets, her hands were placed on top of her chest as if in deep silent prayer. Our mother was a prayer. I knew she prayed to God before her last breath. And she kept secrets. The daughters would never know what secrets our mother kept and took away with her. But there is one thing our mother never took with her or kept a secret, the teachings of wisdom and truth. That was no mystery, but known only to the people who believed. Our mother made believers out of us, even when we swam, thirst, and hungered in her womb. Sometimes, I heard her voice speaking, inside her womb, spreading the teachings, and gathered that my father left us before then. We didn't need his teachings, all we needed was his sperm to make us great. For that, I give my father the glory!

For this morning, on this day, I sit in the woven tent where my mother passed and raised me and my sisters. I write this to other cultures hoping they can hear me, hear us, feel our pain with a kind heart, and multitudes of sympathy, but I once remember our mother telling us sympathy is like one cent.

It adds less alone. But when more than one cent comes together, they make millions. I believe every single word my mother told and taught us, still to this day, I can still hear her.

As I write this in the memory of my mother, and for the courage of our family, our sisters, I reveal much emotions, motives, hardship, pain, struggles, just as much as any other woman in the eyesight of integrity. I reveal the true meaning of My Sisters, Amandla.

We are still here.

I see Amandla standing in the doorway of our woven tent. I would never forget her smile, an artist, a creative person, a powerful woman; brave and strong, the Estonian form of Alice, meaning noble, Precious Jewel or gemstone, or it also has a meaning of warm honey, and love.

I am My Sisters, Amandla.

Short Story and Poems by Imelda Valisto Caravaca

Siopao And Bear Brand Tied With Heartstrings

My Dearest Mother, Virginia

There are times when I find myself missing my mother. I would buy a Bear Brand milk in a can wrapped in white paper with the bear design, heat it and then bite into a siopao. Yes, a siopao. Hot bun in English for you. Cha siu bao in Chinese.

In retrospect, warm milk and siopao isn't the perfect combination. Asado siopao calls for a cold, cold glass of soda. Maybe a glass of Coke or Sarsi. Certainly not milk.

But the memories come rushing, flooding in.

A dirty-white Formica top table. A heavy white saucer for my smoking-hot siopao fresh from the steamer. A warm glass of Bear brand milk. These are the memories that I recall.

It was just me and my mother going to this old Chinese restaurant in Caloocan. I didn't care about the other people in that hole in the wall. I don't remember the servers or the other people who patronised the place. I can't remember the smells that must have wafted from the kitchen. But I recollect the steam from the vats and the loud voices of the cook and the staff, however, I wasn't really minding them that much.

What mattered was me biting into the soft asado siopao with slices of boiled egg inside, dark brown gooey siopao sauce dripping on the sides of my mouth as I hungrily assuaged the hunger pangs in my little tummy. In my mind's eyes, the siopao was a big squishy mound that spelled out "Y-U-M-M-Y!"

I can't call to mind any conversations, if there were any. Maybe there was but it's all forgotten now. But I reminisce my mother sitting across the table vaguely. I cannot recall the way she looked. I can't recall her face. At that time, I was either between the age of four to six. Not remembering the way she looked then kind of upsets me now. I wish I could remember the way she looked then.

I think back to my mother buying me A-line dresses; I particularly love a red polyester pantsuit and my red faux leather clogs. I remember the pair of red clogs very well because it made clippitty-clappity sounds as I walked down the street with my mother.

I hark back on going to the wet market with her and I would gingerly step on the grimy wet floor of the market as she hopped from the fish stalls to the meat stalls bargaining, haggling with the vendors for a fair price. I would be holding on to her dress, careful not to step on the damp floor because the dirty, black water could splash on my legs leaving dark, black streaks on my fair-complexioned legs. It was icky when that would happen.

I look back on the smells in the wet market though – fishy smells so I would breathe through my mouth. But I loved it when once she bought me a miniature red palayok – claypot for you.

Looking back on those memories nostalgically I realised what I didn't know then that she loved me in her own little ways. My mother was not the hugging type but she tied my hair in ponytails with coloured ribbons every time I'd go to school. She was a wonderful cook and the kitchen was always warm and smelled the aroma of the dishes she cooked. She used to cook a mean sinigang sa bayabas, adobo and nilaga, my favourites. My number one love language are words of affirmation; hers were acts of service. I miss her so.

Since Virginia Moved Away

My lips a straight line,
The sky is glumly grey,
It sure feels that way
Since Virginia moved away.

Food tastes like blah,
Rain pours non-stop,
I lost my hooray
Since Virginia moved away.

Light fled in the dark,
I mope in the park ,
I'm not as happy as a lark
Since Virginia moved away.

A Daughter's Lament

Why are there cloudy skies and where does it come from?

And how come rain pours down from the sky?

And why did my mother get ill and die?

The cloudy skies store the torrent of tears

And every drop of rain tells stories of sadness and fear,

Yet I do not know why your mother should suffer and die…

Dearest Nanay

Your name in Latin
Means maiden,
pronounced Vir-JIN-yah.

I never knew
That you were proud of me
Until Ate Bella told me years ago
Before she left for England.

You never told me
That you loved me.
I only knew in hindsight
That your love language
Was acts of service
While mine are words of affirmation.
So for the longest time,
I didn't feel loved,
Until I read
About the Five Languages of Love.

Dear Mom

When I was 4 or 5,
You'd bring me to the wet market.
Once, you brought me a tiny, red clay pot.
I treasured that;
Then as things would have it,
It broke.

Crossing the street,
I saw a little girl my age
With ice cream;
My eyes were drawn to her,
You fished chocolates from your purse,
I looked away from the dripping ice cream.

There would be times
When you'd bring me
To this Chinese hole in the wall resto.
You'd order me a siopao
Paired with a glass of warm milk.
Now, no matter how that pairing
Is not what it should be –
Steamed bun goes better with soda,
When I want to bring back those memories,

I'd buy one *cha sui bao* and warm some milk.
When I was in Grade IV,
I angrily lashed out at you
Because you couldn't afford
To buy me a Hawaiian skirt.

I remember the day
You lamented to my high school besties –
Lydia and Nimia,
You told them,
"My only fault is being poor."

In high school,
My secret dream
Was to be a baton twirler.
(I thought I was prettier than some of them.)
I never spoke of it.

When my Science HS teacher asked me
If I could represent CSNHS,
I declined without telling you.
Our history of poverty
Deprived me of certain chances.

I remember though,
You pulled out all the stops
When I had to attend
A national journalism conference.
You had several blouses sewn,
One was particularly colourful,
Something that I recall fondly.

My BFF Edwin
Always made you laugh,
He'd buy veggies and fish
And the two of you would cook
In our tiny kitchen.
Nanay, I couldn't have chosen
A better friend,
Except that he was the one
Who chose me first
all those years in college.
He's still with me,
A constant companion virtually
Even if we don't meet all the time.
But he treated me and our little family

When I turned 60.
Nanay, in the past
When I prayed to God
That I'm having problems,
I'd see you in a dream looking at me.

You know that I'm going under right now,
Bobbing up and down
In my challenges.
You appeared to me
In your favourite vermillion house dress,
You were also drowning in the water
That is ruler-deep,
Your eyes were closed.
I know that you know.
The water is clear, 12 inches deep,
And it gives me hope.

I know I'll make it through, Nanay
Because you're praying to God.

In my early 20s,
Sad, distant, depressed

Dear Mom

I was, I always admired you
For your spunk, your sense of humour,
Your *joie de vivre*.
Something I'm not.
But later in life;
I've become YOU
Because
I'm my mother's daughter after all.

Nanay, forgive me
For the times
When I answered you back.
The night before you died
Could have been my opportunity
To apologise but I held back
Thinking that I'd have other days.
I was so wrong.

You'd always tell me:
"Strike while the iron is hot."
I never seemed to have perfected that
But I'm getting there.

That night, before God took you back,
You told Mama Pining,
"I've been remiss in my obligations to God."
I realised that it was your confession,
I was listening
But didn't know how to comfort you.
I wish that I knew then what to say.

Nanay, I know we'd be together
But please not so soon.
I choose to do something first
For Gerard and Inno,
Your beloved grandsons.
Until my mission is done,
God will let me stay here on earth
A little bit longer.
Only He knows when He'd bring me home.

Short Story by
Dante Villanueva Aguilar

My Mother's Voice

Mother, mama, mommy, momshie, maderaka,, madir, mudra, nanay, inay, ina, iloy etc.

So many terms of endearment for a woman whose love has no boundaries. An extraordinary individual whose value to everyone's life is beyond description.

A mother's love is a strong foundation of my being. Her care has been my formidable fortress to see the fullness of life. Her understanding makes me experience the beauty this life brings. And her guidance is a guiding force that moulded my being to be the person that l am today.

While Dad's discipline had been my armour, giving me the sense of direction, my mother's affection remains my shield, protecting me against life's endless battles. Her wisdom of old age shall forever be my inspiration in every struggle. I see hope even in defeat and remain humble in every triumph. For her, a great warrior is defined not only on battles won, but also on battles fought.

Yesterday, today and forever - *Mother knows best*

During my early years, when I wasn't yet fully comprehensive of the facets of life, I had so many questions left unanswered. Questions that puzzled me and remain a mystery. I wonder why my Mom would devote her time taking care of the poor, the orphan, the sick and the dying. People who are totally strangers abandoned by their families and would find shelter in our small home. In her simple and modest way she gave them comfort and shared even a portion of our meals. All these without expecting anything in return. She shed tears for every passing of a dying orphan she cared for. Same tears she'd give to an abandoned person reunited with loved ones and have to say goodbye to return to their homes. Sad, but also happy knowing that these people had finally found a home to live, a family to be with.

Now I fully understand the reasons behind it. Mom once told me that we shall live only once in this world and we do not hold what is in store for our future. So any goodness or kindness that we want to share, let it be today. Not tomorrow nor next time, or some other time. The best time is now for we are uncertain of what is up for tomorrow. Let tomorrow not consume your time today. We are created in the likeness of our

Creator with a heart ready and knows how to love. It is but fitting that even in simple things and opportunities we can share such goodness to those who are in dire need so they too shall be able to experience the beauty this life brings. For a simple act of goodness brings hope to the hopeless, gives smiles to those who are weary and comfort to those who are desperate.

For Mom, there is no greater pain for someone than being abandoned, forgotten and forsaken by their loved ones. Much more if time, money and care were spent for that loved one that when they are now successful from their chosen fields, become ingratitude to those who supported them.

I had made a vow to myself that this will never happen to Mom. For as long as my strength allows me, I shall be a pillar of hope for Mom. An assurance that gives my Mom serenity within because she will never be alone in her sunset years.

Now and Forever, her unconditional love will always be my source of strength and inspiration. Her guiding voice allows me to appreciate the goodness this life brings. Her loving care allows me to experience the fullness of life. Her sacrifices allowed me to understand that every trial that comes my way is allowed by God. Because He has reasons for everything. Even if trials seem beyond my understanding, I should never doubt God's goodness. Because it is during our lowest moment that we come closest to God. That the best moment to mould us is how we withstand all the storms along our journey. Braving all storms with expectant faith in the Almighty gives substance to our hope that makes us certain of the realities we do not see.

There is no greater pain for a mother grieving for the loss of her love at the time that she was not yet ready to handle life alone. With the death of my dad, my mom's first and only love, she was left alone taking care of her four children. During her weakest point, I saw a mother of great faith, a fierce warrior who refuses to be defeated by any form of pain and sacrifice. Alone, she fought the battle, offering her time and effort to protect us and secure our future. She wrestled even the strongest storm to secure us from harm and from all sorts of pains.

For mom, the deaths of dad, her only love; Manang Josephine, her eldest child and Jorey, her eldest grandson are pages of life that no matter how much it hurts she has to endure and accept life's painful reality. Behind those tears as manifestation of grief is a strong woman who is standing tall amidst all the trials and sufferings.

In more than three decades of my struggle to be able to rise up to the challenges of life, I reached a point of decision finding my way home. Mom is getting old and already in her dawning years at the age of 82. At this time, she already needs someone to guide her in her old age. At the crossroads of my life there is a need to choose: continue to spread my wings and explore the limitless horizon of opportunities or go home to a simple life by my mother's side. I have chosen what my heart whispers rather than what my mind commands. Mom is nearing her sunset years and only a few more years to enjoy life. I can longer take chances being away from her when the time comes that she shall need me the most.

In my mom's loving arms I found comfort and assured her that I can take care of her at all times. Her strength is no longer the same as it was before. Her steps are no longer as fast as they used to be. And her frail body moulded by hardship and hard work can no longer be relied upon being alone.

This prompted me to set aside my quest for greatness in a faraway place and make a fresh start besides my mom. Covid 19 had been instrumental for me to see the realities this life brings. Had to concede to my mom's request to stay while the pandemic was still around. She thinks of my welfare more than hers. Indeed a mother's love is beyond description, it's boundless, it's immense.

My Mom's advice had been my fortress and strength in life's struggles – taking chances despite the failures experienced; never giving up no matter how bleak the future. Life even of its uncertainties is still a beautiful life, worth living. Yes, there are moments of confusion and delusions. So many questions remained unanswered. The quest for greatness seems unending. The accolades, recognitions, applauses are sights to behold, sweet music to hear and fondest memories to recall. But to whom these victories and success are for if we neglect the chance to give back the love and care to our parents, especially our mom who all along had been part of our success.

In her sleep, once again I took a glance at my Mom. I could see on her face that peace and contentment from her smile even if in deep sleep. Not like during those last nights as I prepared back to Manila where sorrow and anxiety were evident in Mom's sleep. It would take a couple of nights for my Mom to be composed once again worrying about my situation being alone in a place away from home.

I held Mom's wrinkled hands. The thick callus from her hands were testaments of a long hardship, a never ending struggle to life. Never had I seen her give up on any challenge of life. Perhaps because her faith strengthened her. When I placed her hands on my cheek, suddenly I felt her loving care. Her caring hands had been a guiding force in my every journey so as not to go astray along the way. Mom is my oasis, my sanctuary.

Time passes and time wasted can no longer be relieved and revisited. While regrets happen at the end, we can avoid being sorry if we know from the start what is right and just. Despite all the opportunities awaiting me in the big city, I have chosen this time to stay with my Mom here in the province. A decision I long thought of after more than three decades of quest to greatness in the corporate world where success is lord and survival of the toughest is law. The asphalt jungle follows the law of the land where opportunism is the standard operation. It's now time to choose what comes close to my heart – what gives more meaning to life. Time is of the essence, and every single moment with my Mom is a precious moment spent. Yes this shall be a new leash of life for me, taking a fresh start for a new career. There may be some apprehensions, but knowing that I now have the chance to take care of my Mom would be a blessing while I am starting my career in a place I call home.

For a moment I shall not hear the applause, no longer be part of the gatherings, and just a spectator giving applause to the achievers. I had my share of the limelight. Taking the sidelight momentarily is no big deal. I know soon I shall be able to once again attain success at the right time at the right opportunity. It is just a matter of time as long as you never stop dreaming, you never cease believing and you never give up taking chances – the stairway to success is right at your doorsteps.

All these years, Mother's love is magical – so pure and immaculate. So unconditional and limitless. Her love reminds me to always keep my feet on the ground no matter how high I fly when I spread my wings so wide to explore the boundless horizon of opportunities. Her advice always reminds me to remain humble no matter how great success is achieved. For a person will be well remembered not of his success, but of his significance.

As we grow older, our priorities change. My siblings already have their own circle of friends and acquaintances. They have their own family to take care of and separate responsibilities to attend to. An ageing Mom is now at the sidelight. Her opinion no longer matters for her grandchildren. Her presence is hardly felt and her help is no longer sought. In most of the outings she is left alone at home. She may oftentimes conceal her pain, but her eyes betray her sadness. Behind those bitter smiles is sadness that she tried to hide from others.

Each of us have callings: some for matrimony, others for priesthood and mine for single-blessedness. This was never an option but a personal choice. I know this is my purpose of living to be with my Mom every special moment of her life. Giving her assurance that in her sunset years shall be by her side to comfort and take care of her, just the way she did during my childhood.

Her wisdom of old age is beyond description as this was derived from her past experience. Her words of wisdom, no matter how repetitive, continue to be of great value. Maybe because this was etched from pain, struggle, triumph and trials of life.

Wherever my success leads me to, **my mother's voice** will always lead me home. Her guidance shall serve as a light to my path in the midst of darkness. Reminding me always that life is beautiful, that it holds many blessings. We only need to experience its goodness and sadness to be able to appreciate its fullness. In a world so filled with hatred and vindictiveness, a mother's love radiates like a diamond. It is precious and pure. No limitations, no beginning and no end. A mother's love endures all pains. It is willing to love even if it hurts some more. It loves even more until it hurts no more.

We often forget that while we are so busy chasing dreams – taking leaps and bounds, our dear parents in their old age are catching up to be at pace with us. But most of the time they are left behind. Their old age prevents them from doing so.

If during our childhood they had been our source of strength, now that their strength fails them, let us become their pillars of strength. May our voices be their guide, when their eyesight can no longer lead them the way. Let us be their guiding force, their sanctuary and their oasis when they can no longer stand the test of time in their dawning moments. When we look back upon our life, the moments that stand out in our memory are moments shared with our parents, especially our mother. She has a heart with unconditional love that never loses hope. Always believing in the promises of love no matter how many times she may have been hurt and discouraged. She may not be perfect, but her love is – willing to sacrifice and bear all the pains to protect her children.

It is my prayer that till the end of time, we will not neglect them and be their companion as they welcome every sunrise and await every sunset until they can no longer see both. For every chapter of their lives, you, me, we – their children comprise every page of their life yesterday, today and till the end of time.

Short Story by
Maitrayee Banerjee

The Scent Of Kurchi
(Translated by Sayar Banerjee)

"Can't you sit like a proper woman? How many times do I have to tell you? If you sit with your legs spread like that you would be married so far away that you won't be by your mother's side when she dies." Mitul's cantankerous aunt spews these words against her before traipsing back to the kitchen.

Mitul is four years old and does not possess any understanding of death. In her blissful innocence, she grasps the very idea as becoming stars up in heaven. However, even imagining her mother being a star way up in the sky, far away from her, terrifies Mitul. She readily rectifies her sitting posture while ruminating on her breakfast. Needless to mention, "sitting properly" does not apply to Mitul's male cousins who can sit however and wherever they want…no one is going to take them away from their mothers.

No women in the house are allowed in the sanctum sanctorum where the paterfamilias reside, so they need to eat and sleep in the kitchen and a few small rooms adjacent to the kitchen. Mitul also stays there with her mother, although she does not get a hold of her very often, except at night during sleep. Even that time is not long enough as her mother rises very early in the morning in order to prepare for the worshipping rituals. When the first light of dawn appears, she searches for her mother beside her and cries out in her absence.

"Shut up, you little demon! Your mother hasn't croaked yet! She's just outside plucking flowers," shouts her grandma.

Everyone loves to allude to death in this house. Even though the little ones don't grasp its meaning, its mere mention is enough to silence them.

Back in the day, the front entrance of most country houses used to remain open. No one prevented anyone from going out or coming in. But there wasn't also any fear of thievery. One can say that people used to have a moral compass during that time, unlike now. Trust for each other was also abound and it wasn't a sign of weakness or naiveté. Mitul and other kids like her could play around without any inhibition and they enjoyed it. One day, however, Mitul finds that very front door to be shut. Utterly perplexed, she tries to find her parents and other adults in the house.

Finally, she finds all of them on the roof, eagerly watching a spectacle taking place in the front yard. The spectacle is the public lynching of a young adult by some political goons. Funny, isn't it? I was just talking about the blissful idyllic life of the good old days. The young man's crime is that he spoke out against a totalitarian government in power. Seeing him getting beaten to a pulp, Mitul cries out in anguish and terror. Her grandma tries to smother her scream. Mitul's mother, on the other hand, is not a woman who would just be a bystander. She comes down the stairs, opens the door, and stands up to the monsters beating on the young man. Mitul never saw that much anger in her mother's eyes ever again. The monsters, who are basically cowards, recognize that anger and leave the young man alone. Mitul always loved her mother. But that day, an altar was created in her mind for her.

A few years down the road. Mitul is now prancing around a picturesque mountain river. There is not much water. The sky is clear and cerulean. The air is pristine. Mitul looks genuinely happy. She is accompanied by Ratul, a handsome young man. The river bank and the surroundings are verdant with a diverse range of plant species. Mitul recognizes one of the flowers among them – Kurchi (*Holarrhena pubescens*). She used to pluck these small white flowers and wear them as a nose-ring back in her village. The sudden surge of memories brings a winsome smile on her face.

"Why're you smiling?" Ratul asks her.

"You won't understand," she replies.

"Why women do what they do, I'll never understand," Ratul comments.

Mitul smiles again looking at him. There is sadness hidden under the veneer of that gleeful smile.

Mitul had to leave her village for better opportunities and a better education when she was eight. As Mitul's mother did most of the household chores, in her absence the in-laws started facing the brunt of that responsibility. As a consequence, Mitul's mother was blamed viciously by them as an opportunist and disruptor. Moreover, the in-laws did not think about holding back their criticism even in front of Mitul. Despite leaving, Mitul continued to visit her village a few times a year. But soon, she found it difficult to recognize as the big family kept fragmentising, and the skirmishes between the in-laws seemed like a perennial event. Eventually, Mitul's friendship with her childhood friend fell victim to this as well. Even today, she still doesn't understand why every adult relationship is fraught with so much unwarranted complicacy. As time passed, the distance between Mitul's old home and the new one widened – both physically and emotionally.

"Why do you still sit so formally, mum?" Rooney asks her mother quite often.

"It's just a habit," replies Mitul.

Rooney lives abroad. Every night she calls her mother and talks about her day. Sometimes she allows her son to talk to her grandma across the pond. Mitul never tried to make Rooney a proper woman like her aunts did with her. She wonders if Rooney would be by her side when she finally leaves this world. She tried so hard to hold on to her own mother and yet when she was placed under assisted ventilation, Mitul could not be there. She wasn't there when her mother took her last breath despite being a proper and mild-mannered woman for her entire life. When Mitul was a kid, a popular song about finding someone's mother used to make her bawl regularly. When she became an adult, the bawling stopped but the fear of losing her was still there.

Nowadays she sees her mother every day, in her dreams. She embraces her and inhales her scent, just like the scent of Kurchi. For a while she forgets that she and her mother belong to different worlds now. When she wakes up, she waits for the path to get to the other side…the path to become a star above in the firmament. Mother is waiting for her there. She knows now that no destination is far away, it's just a matter of time.

Poem by Riddhima Sen

Rose Petals

Dear mom,
Thanks for making life liveable
And for always staying by my side through thick and thin;
I still remember the time when you stayed up,
Throughout the night
To look after me.
When I was down with a high fever
You never let me realise how sad you were,
But always made me laugh when I used to cry.

It's hard to be there for others,
When you are broken from the inside.
How hard is it to sacrifice your dreams
For your child,
Maybe, only mothers know how to do so.
They love us unconditionally,
The purest bond in the world
Comes into existence
Because moms exist.

God created mothers
To protect children on his behalf
And love them abound.

Poem by Nivedita Bhattacharya

Where The Phoenix Transcends…

God created the world in seven days,
That's what the mythology says;
The logical minds, however, debate that it was
Big Bang that led to the cellular ways.

But if you ask me,
Which is the ultimate force behind Genesis…
It would be without a doubt "You," my mother,
Who brought me into the world's premises.

Right from the moment of conceiving me,
To the day of my birth, and thereon;
It has been you, who has diligently protected me
By plucking away my promenade's thorns.

As a toddler when I was still trying to
Figure out how to walk;
You had it all figured out and were ready
To sacrifice anything to compose my life's melodious orch.

Dear Mom

T'was my first stage appearance when I was three,
And hell knows how nervous was I;
But one look at you was enough to
Bid all my apprehensions goodbye.

I still remember the day I first bled,
Confused, scared… Oh! It was a full mayhem;
But you held my hand and said, "It was alright,
We're women, we bleed every month, and we are born ready to slay them."

Whether it was my first kiss, my first failure, or my heartbreaks,
You have always been my life's constant;
With you I could be completely open and speak my heart out,
'Cause you never judged me, even when I was despondent.

You were my first teacher, my first fashion icon,
My best friend, and the list goes on;
You taught me how to face the world with a smile,
And how to overcome the hurdles by mocking them: "Oh C'mon!"

Today I am an adult, I live my life on my own terms,

And yes, I do fight with you like a maniac;

But still, no matter what, deep down I know,

You will always be the haven where I can crawl safely back.

Some people say Phoenix is a myth, some call it a legend,

I won't know, because of course, I have never seen it;

But if phoenix symbolises "life after death" and stands for transformation,

My phoenix is "You" – my source of determination and grit.

Everytime I fell down, everytime life kicked me in the gut,

More than me, it was you who developed the scars;

You sheltered me within your protective wings,

Burst into flames like a phoenix and destroyed the tyrant czars.

It is said that a phoenix burns itself down and is reborn,

You've burned, not once but, again and again, to ensure that I ascend;

You have rekindled the dead fire within me,

Dear mother, because of you today I am yet another phoenix who is ready to transcend.

Poem by Quinn Jam

Marina's Lullaby

A woman's body –
One of God's greatest creations,
A unique masterpiece with lots of wonders,

Perfectly crafted with the ability to carry another life –
It deserves an innate respect and significance.
Thus, being a mother like you is one next level woman.

"Out on the ocean sailing away
I can hardly wait
To see you come of age
But I'll guess we'll both just have to be patient
'Cause it's a long way to go."

From the first day I was conceived
I may have heard you speak your daily thoughts,
I may have shared your emotions and mood swings,
I may have felt your urge to cradle me in your arms.

The joy of hearing the beat of my heart,
The thumping of my feet in your womb,
The amazing responses with every touch
Are cherished memories while you patiently wait…

Until the day I was finally out and burst my first cry,
I felt the overflowing joy and excitement,

I knew that I was carefully taken care of
With your strong will and love.

Giving birth doesn't end your responsibilities –
Many sleepless nights and tireless days were spent,
Like an endless job, you helped me make it through,
You made sure I was given the right amount of care.

Your own condition isn't your priority anymore,
Postpartum care may have been neglected;
Being the mindful and overprotective you
I am nursed exceptionally with your extra attention.

A hard row to hoe,
Yes, it's a long way to go,
But in the meantime,
Before you cross the street,
Take my hand.

I couldn't imagine how hard it is sometimes
To care for the family and for yourself at the same time.
A mother's touch is incomparable to that of Midas,

Your love and affection is priceless.

I am your first but being a mother of eight is exceptional.

I'm still in awe of how you had us all through normal delivery.

Most of the time, you're the only one who have guided us,

Your bravery, compassion and determination are indeed amazing.

Being a first-time mom, I became part of your daily routine,

You fed me healthy food to grow up fast,

You changed my clothes to make me comfortable

And you taught me how to be an accomplished child.

Step by step, word by word

You were the first one to witness

My little accomplishments as a child,

You were always there to guide me unconditionally.

Then I started going to school,

I finally took my first learning to practise.

I remembered how you taught me to read and write,

That's why my famous long name was never a bother to me.

You always encouraged me to excel in my own way,
To be the best version of myself year after year.
It's a lot of challenge and pressure for a child like me
But I always aim to make you prouder every time.

Row, Row, Row your boat
Gently down the stream,
Merrily, merrily, merrily, merrily
Life is but a dream.

You're multi-talented and multi-tasked,
Doing chores while teaching me is your game
Anything you do with your hands comes out creatively
Everything you do is amazing and passionate.

Your trust and confidence in my ability made me one of the best.
You made me meet new friends and broaden my horizon,

I became a victor because of the motivation and inspiration,

Seeing you happy after each award is my reward.

Life without you will be a complete mess.

Together, we will row the boat of life

Until I can finally provide you

The greatest dream you have ever desired for me – my success.

When the blazing sun is gone, when nothing shines upon me,
Then you show your little light, twinkle, twinkle, all night.
Twinkle, twinkle, little star how I wonder what you are!
Then the traveller in the dark thanks you for your tiny spark,
How could he see where to go, if you did not twinkle so?

Side by side, we walked the graduation aisle with flying colours

With the snapshot of our next goal – to reach greater heights,

With the undying support and positivity

You have bestowed me wisdom and guidance.

The urge of the city's lights and glamour

Called upon me, like a promised land I should seek,
My curiosity and self-entitlement made me forget
That I'm leaving you home, for the first time.

I strived to be as independent and determined as I can be,
I managed to settle myself for years without your help,
I accomplished things on my own despite struggles,
I survived the city jungle only a few rural people tried to conquer.

Years passed, I only visited you when time permitted me.
Though I missed you cook my favourite meals,
I lived alone in this busy, crowded city
But it doesn't lead me to where I really want to be…

We both have become tired and exhausted –
You tending to my father's and siblings' daily needs,
Me struggling to make ends meet here,
Then the pandemic happened…

As devastated and lonely as others,

I was left alone here without any chance to go home.
Travel and health restrictions have been imposed,
I couldn't go to you, I just couldn't leave here.

Problems started to arise one by one,
With situations which triggered my insanity.
It was the start of my darkest days,
I couldn't feel any hope to move forward.

Everything became confusing,
Tomorrow became unclear and plans have changed.
We lost some of our friends and loved ones,
Depression eats up my personal space.

I was lost in my dark, long journey,
It felt that I have been alone for the longest time,
I didn't even notice that my will to connect has drifted apart.
Then I realised I need you and God's light to save me.

Though time created that invincible gap between us,
It felt like I left home just yesterday.
I was welcomed back with your warmth and grace;

You, as God's instrument, have lightened up my path again.

A dream is a wish your heart makes.
When you're fast asleep,
In dreams you will lose your heartaches.
Whatever you wish for, you keep,
Have faith in your dreams, and someday
Your rainbow will come smiling through.
No matter how your heart is grieving,
If you keep on believing
The dream that you wish will come true.

You helped me bring back the radiant and adventurous me,

You reached my hand from falling off that dark cliff,

You have forgiven me for every time we lost from being apart,

You have showered me back the love and attention I have longed so much.

Now my direction has been cleared up again,

You took me back to where I was once lost.

My faith and burning desire to accomplish fresh goals are back,

I started to be grateful again to the precious life I still have.

Thank you for not leaving me in my darkest times,

Thank you for always standing still and staying strong beside us,

Thank you for being the best mom we could ever ask for,

Thank you for taking care of your health for us.

Thank you for being the embodiment of a great mother.

We appreciate all of your sacrifices for us when we have nothing,

We understand your pain and struggle to be with us,

We are deeply grateful for staying alive and be treated from your sickness.

You may think we have not heard you cry in the middle of the night,

That we may not know how hard you fought your silent battles too,

That we may not have felt your regrets and discontentment,

We understand you're a super mom but still a human.

I'm sorry for all the frustration and disappointments,

I'm sorry for making you wait for so long before we can come home,

I'm sorry for having you and dad eat alone without us,

I'm sorry for bearing the weight of being alone at home when we're not around.

I promise to make you prouder again this time,

I promise to travel with you to all the places we couldn't reach,

I promise to give you your dream garden and pets,

I promise to be the best version of a daughter you can always be proud of.

"And still so many things I want to say.
Remember all the songs you sang for me,
When we went sailing on an emerald bay
And like a boat out on the ocean,
I'm rocking you to sleep.

The water's dark and deep, inside this ancient heart,
You'll always be a part of me.
Goodnight, my angel, now it's time to dream,
And dream how wonderful your life will be.
Someday your child may cry, and if you sing this lullaby,
Then in your heart there will always be a part of me.
Someday we'll all be gone,
But lullabies go on and on,
They never die,
That's how you and I will be."

Yes, I have come of age to be the next mother,

However I may not have been gifted the womb to bear a child.

It's sad that I may not be able to fulfil and accomplish what you did

But I'm still proud I'll always remain as one of your babies.

We still have long years ahead of us.

Please stay as cheerful and strong as you are now,

So you can still wear pretty heels in my wedding day

And play, dine and travel with your grandchildren too.

We will stay twinning our favourite outfits,

Eat everything we both crave for,

Visit places that will give us calm and peace,

Then we go shopping to satisfy your heart's material desires.

Though I may not have the chance to be a mother like you,

I would always wonder how you did it all through those years.

I would always dream of becoming another you as a mother,

I would always hope to be your daughter again in our next lives.

No words could really fathom how happy and grateful I am

Having been blessed with your purity and endearing presence.

I always wish you a long, peaceful and healthy life,

So, forever we'll hear the sweetness of your voice while singing your lullabies.

Credits to creators of these lullaby songs:
"Beautiful Boy (Darling Boy)"

"Row, Row, Row Your Boat"
"Twinkle, Twinkle, Little Star"
"A Dream is a Wish Your Heart Makes"
"Lullaby (Goodnight, My Angel)"

Short Story by R. Chaitanya

The Mother

Gayatri was the central point of her small and loving family. Her son Akhil, daughter-in-law, Smita and naughty Mishti were the apples of her eyes. She had no complaints and regrets except one that her husband had left them very early.

Mishti had a deep love for her grandmother, who was the most important person in her life. Mishti's parents were busy with work and other responsibilities, so her grandmother was the one who took care of her most of the time. Mishti's grandmother was a kind, gentle woman who had a wealth of knowledge about life and the world around her. She loved spending time with Mishti and would often tell her stories about their ancestors and their culture. Mishti was fascinated by her grandmother's stories and would listen intently to every word she said.

Mishti was Gayatri's favourite companion. Both of them used to spend all their time together. She was always with her grandmother – playing, studying, doing homework, painting, dancing. They were best friends. Life was flowing very smoothly. Every day her grandmother would take her to the park where she would play on the swings, climb on the jungle gym, and run around with other children.

One sunny afternoon, Mishti's grandmother decided to take her to a different park that was a little farther away. Mishti was excited and couldn't wait to explore the new park. They set out on their journey, chatting and holding hands as they walked. As they were crossing a busy street, Mishti suddenly pulled her hand away from her grandmother's grip and ran ahead, chasing a butterfly. Her grandmother called out to her to come back, but Mishti was too engrossed in the chase. Suddenly, a speeding car came out of nowhere and hit Mishti, throwing her several feet away. Her grandmother screamed in horror as she saw her little granddaughter lying motionless on the road. People rushed to help, and Mishti was taken to the hospital, but it was too late. She had suffered severe head injuries and passed away that evening.

Mishti's family was devastated by her sudden and tragic death. Her grandmother blamed herself for letting go of her hand and not being able to protect her. The accident left a permanent scar on her heart. Mishti's parents struggled to come to terms with their loss and were haunted by the thought of what could have been if only they had been more careful. It deeply devastated the poor mother who had lost her only child. It affected her intensely. She left her job and would spend all her day in Mishti's room.

She was shattered. She couldn't believe that her little angel was no more. Smita started to suffer from depression and anxiety. She would often have panic attacks, and her sleep patterns were disturbed. She would cry for hours, remembering the times she spent with her daughter. Her husband and family tried to console her, but nothing seemed to work. Days turned into weeks, and weeks turned into months, but Smita's condition only worsened. She stopped going to work and stopped talking to anyone. She would sit in her room, looking at Mishti's photographs and talking to her as if she was still there. Her husband decided to take her to a psychiatrist. The psychiatrist diagnosed Smita with severe depression and prescribed medication and therapy. But, even after taking medication, Smita's mental health continued to deteriorate. She would often hallucinate and see Mishti's ghost. She would talk to Mishti and even try to feed her food.

One day, while Smita was in her room, she heard Mishti's voice calling her. She ran towards the voice and jumped out of the window, hoping to meet her daughter. She was badly injured and had to be hospitalised. Her husband and mother-in-law realised that Smita needed specialised care, and they admitted her to a mental health facility. Smita was diagnosed with severe schizophrenia and was given intensive treatment. This made Gayatri's life terrible, she felt suffocated over the loss. Both the mother and son had realised that Smita's condition would worsen whenever she was in front of her. It was heart-wrenching for poor Gayatri. The burden of guilt was eating her deeply down. She made a decision. She gathered her courage to tell her decision to go to Shanti Niketan. It was another bolt out of the blue for poor Akhil. He was in a complete head-scratching situation. Both of them decided to depart in the early morning.

At 5:15 am, Gayatri was ready to depart to her destination. Perplexed, Akhil was not in a position to say yes or no. They weren't talking. She fell asleep in the car and when she woke up and looked around she saw a big board on which was written: SHANTI NIKETAN – OLD-AGE HOME. She stood quiet with tears in her eyes. Akhil was taking out all of her belongings from the car. He then walked towards the reception and asked for Mr. Mehta. The receptionist called Mr. Mehta immediately. They greeted each other.

Akhil said, "Sir, please meet my mother. I talked about her with you yesterday."

Mr. Mehta was the manager of the old age home. He bade Gayatri a good morning and respectfully took her to her room. An employee brought along her suitcase and bags. Akhil did not come. Gayatri felt like running back and hugging her son, but she stopped herself, because she knew that it would hurt Akhil more and then it would be very difficult to go back for him. So, she gathered herself and slipped quietly into her new abode.

Around ninety elderly people lived there. For the whole day, she kept herself completely confined in her room, and did not come for breakfast or lunch. When Mr. Mehta came to know about this, he sent Karuna to call her for dinner. Gayatri came down and met everyone. Gradually, she became a friend to everyone.

One day she asked Mr. Mehta, "Can I contribute in any way? I would be highly obliged if you could let me help you."

"Sure, madam. I will definitely let you know," Mr. Mehta said.

She started to take interest in gardening, the kitchen and other things, as if it were her own home.

She would give useful tips to the cook and the gardener. She had a good knowledge of gardening. After two months, everybody was astonished to see that the whole ground was full of beautiful flowers. Even vegetables were being grown and used in the kitchen. In the kitchen, nutritious things were made in a way that everybody loved to eat. Everyone was happy that they were eating the vegetables grown in their own old age home. Gayatri became everybody's favourite. Whenever someone was ill, she was the first person to go and take care of him/her. After three months, she was appointed the Chief Coordinator of the old age home. She was the happiest person there, even though she missed Mishti, Smita and Akhil a lot. After Mr. Mehta passed away, she took up charge of the old age home. Her decisions were always respected, and gradually, SHANTI NIKETAN became an ideal place for old people.

After two years, Akhil came to meet her with Smita. The three of them had their respective guilts and pains in their hearts. Both Akhil and Smita were happy to see the new avatar of their mother. They were proud of her. Gayatri was happy with her decision to live in the old age home as she knew that Smita would never be normal in her presence. Smita asked her to pack her bags and come back home but Gayatri denied. Smita expressed her guilt that because of her Gayatri had to leave her home.

Tears rolled down her cheeks, Gayatri hugged her lovingly and said, "No, my child. I understood your pain well. I am also a mother. It was not your fault. It was your pain over the loss of your only child, nothing else. I am equally happy here as now I am the proud mother of ninety children here, I am not at loss. I am blessed."

About the Authors

Pabitra Adhikary

Pabitra Adhikary, an educator by profession, is the founder of Pabitra Sir Classes, a well-known CAT GMAT preparation institute in Kolkata. Pabitra is not only a dedicated faculty but also a passionate writer. He has written hundreds of poems, stories, articles, science fiction, comics etc. He writes about human relationships, adventures, nature and a human's relationship with nature. He has been published in several mediums and his books are available in Apple Books, Google Play Books, Amazon Audible, Storytel, Kobo, Audiobooks.com, Scribd etc. He also penned the *Adventures of Camelia* series, which was published periodically in Shuktara, a famous Bengali monthly magazine in Kolkata.

Tamikio L. Dooley

Tamikio L. Dooley is an award-winning author who writes fiction and nonfiction of crime, thriller, mystery, fantasy, zombie apocalypse, historical, romance, western and paranormal. In her spare time, she writes poetry, short stories, articles, essays, health books, children books, diaries, journals and inspiring books. Tamikio has received awards and certificates for her short stories, poetry, essays, and articles published in Ukiyoto Publishing anthologies, *Bard's Day Key* anthology, *Magazinehorsowar* Magazine, *CreatiVIngenuitiy*, *E-Connections* Magazine, *Multinational* Magazine and *Multinational Pen Soldiers* anthology. Tamikio received an award for outstanding consultant issued by Ukiyoto Publishing and an honourable recognition as the best crime author in September 2016. She's the winner of the World Literature Awards, and won her first crystal trophy award in the crime category.

Imelda Valisto Caravaca

Imelda is a Swiftie, Potterhead, school paper adviser, Principal, textbook writer, the national trainer of NEAP and FUSE, retired supervisor, educator and student for life and an Indie author. She's a part of Ukiyoto's *Chocolate and Petals II* and *Magkasintahan 2.0 XIII* anthologies. A.B. Sociology grad of Bicol U. M.A. Reading grad of the University of the Philippines. Currently, she's a LiSQuP scholar of the Philippine Normal University taking up doctorate studies in Educational Leadership and Management. She self-published *The Moment I Knew I'm So Into You*, her first book of poetry. Currently, she's finishing her memoir *Second Chances for Bipolar Women: Coming Out of the Dark, a Life Under Construction.*

Dante Villanueva Aguilar

Dante is a licensed real estate broker. He's a graduate of Bachelor of Science in Commerce, major in Business Management CUM LAUDE. He's a multi-awarded writer in English, Filipino and Hiligaynon languages. A book Author, novelist, columnist and scriptwriter and a member of the Screenwriters Guild of the Philippines and Sumakwelan Iloilo, Inc. He's a 2022 Grand Prize winner of FWD P100K Self Love Story in English. He was also awarded the "Emerging Author of the Year" by Ukiyoto Publishing in 2022.

Maitrayee Banerjee

Maitrayee Banerjee is an accomplished author, reciter, singer, and voice actor. She spent her life in a small village until the age of eight and thereafter moved near Kolkata for better education. She completed her Master's degree in History from the University of Calcutta. She also has a diploma in music, specialising in the songs written by Rabindranath Tagore. Despite being a homemaker for most of her life, she began pursuing various avenues of artistic expressions which led her to publishing a couple of short story books (*Megh Brishti Roddur* and *Chhoto Golpo Sankalan*) as well as performing in various programmes.

Riddhima Sen

Riddhima Sen is currently studying in Jadavpur University, Kolkata. She is an introvert who likes to read books and write poetry. She even likes to design garments and exciting apparels. She is a Social Media Intern at Younity, a volunteer at Hamari Pahchan NGO, a curriculum-writing intern at Team Everest and the Vice President of the Architecture Club – SUPROS. She desires to enjoy life to the fullest and wants to try every activity under the sun. She likes to recite poems and compose lyrics as well. By participating in leadership programs, she has overcome her introversion to a great extent.

Nivedita Bhattacharya

A musician at heart and writer by passion, Nivedita has a penchant for storytelling and miming, delivering stories creatively to suit different audiences and mediums. She has a decade long experience in working as a marketeer and curating stories for B2B and B2C brands across diverse industries. Apart from her love for music and writing, Nivedita is also an animal right activist and dreams of starting a Stray Rescue Society of her own.

Quinn Jam

Quinn Jam has been a writer since her elementary days. She was a delegate in 2004 NSPC. She excelled as a consistent Editor In Chief and finished College as Cum Laude. She has taken part in various publications even in her first job as Marketing Assistant. She's part of the famous Valentines Anthology – Magkasintahan 2.0 Volume IX. She loves reading novels and watching series which might be useful to her writer's imagination. For her, we should always get the best out of our lives for we might not remember when our next is.

Connect with her via Tiktok or Instagram: *@quinn_jam*

R. Chaitanya

R. Chaitanya is an emerging author. She published four books in 2022. In addition, she has contributed short stories in different editions. She is very passionate about theatre, movies, dance and music. An experimenter by nature, she is full of life and loves to enjoy "now." Her life's mission is to spread love and serenity to people who are in pain and have lost all hopes. In all of her writings, she ends with a positive note for life. "Making best out of waste" is her forte. She strongly believes that there is always a way however dark it may be.

www.ingramcontent.com/pod-product-compliance
Lightning Source LLC
LaVergne TN
LVHW041539070526
838199LV00046B/1740